In Full Bloom

Give Me Flowers So That I Can Live

Arnell Evans, LCDC, CART

BALBOA.PRESS
A DIVISION OF HAY HOUSE

Balboa Press books may be ordered through booksellers or by contacting:

Balboa Press
A Division of Hay House
1663 Liberty Drive
Bloomington, IN 47403
www.balboapress.com
844-682-1282

Print information available on the last page.

ISBN: 979-8-7652-4911-6 (sc)
ISBN: 979-8-7652-4910-9 (e)

Library of Congress Control Number: 2024901215

Balboa Press rev. date: 01/26/2024

DEDICATION

To my husband, Edward "Bert" Evans, III, my soulmate, who walks this journey with me, to LaKeisha Renee "Cricket" our angel, to whom this book could not have been written; to our children and grandchildren who are living proof of this book; "In Full Bloom"

ACKNOWLEDGEMENTS

A very special thanks to my spiritual sister/friend and Author, Frenetta Tate, to my BFF and Author, Sally Green, whose editorial touch is evident on every page in this book.

CONTENTS

THE FLOWER GARDEN

These pages echo Arnell's journey from desolation to empowerment. The art of giving flowers stands as a testament to the beauty that arises from compassion and connection. You are invited to embrace the power of transformation, weaving the art of giving flowers into their own lives and creating their own flower Garden of love and appreciation. The journey's lessons inspire the awakening of their own inner gardens, blooming with resilience, empowerment, hope and the enduring beauty of giving.

Inspirational Prayer:

Heavenly Father you are the Alpha and Omega, the first and the last
You are the creator of the universe the maker of heaven and earth, You are the of God all things seen and unseen, You are light in the darkness a refuge for the weary and a stronghold for the weak
Your majesty fills the heavens, Your glory fills the earth, Today I seek your presence make your presence known to me Father, God, Lord, and King. Holy Spirit you are the one who formed me who knows every thought in my mind every beat of my heart and every detail of my life.

My Inspirations:

Parents, Grandparents, Eddie and Arnella Vinson Sr, Lawrence & Ethel Edwards Sr, Supervisors, Mentors, Sponsors, Books and writings by best known speakers and authors such as Dr. Charles Stanley, Wayne Dyer, Louise Hay, Maya Angelo, Claudia Black, Melanie Beatty, Iylana Van Zant, Jen Sincero, Pastors, Teachers, Gospel and R &B songs. Too many to name.

FOREWORD

by Dr. Shirley Rose-Gilliam

Life after the pandemic has proven to be different. People are in search of what they lost: friends, family, celebrations, stability, time and the list go on. As a retired educator, I received a call from the TRS (Teacher Retirement System of Texas) office asking if I would participate in a mental health survey. I never really thought about my mental health until I experienced it in my family. I didn't know what to say or do. First, I tried to make sense of it and decided to pray it away. We sought professional help and used medication-assisted treatment. Yes, medication would work … praying would work. Everything would be fine. At least I thought. *The date was August 18, 2016. One night, I received a phone call that was very disturbing.*

Two years later, I was hired to provide administrative coaching to a public school. The superintendent of the school was a colleague of mine (we worked together back in 2008). The superintendent knew my story and told me he wanted me to meet someone. As we were walking around the building, he introduced me to Ms. Evans. He spoke highly of her counseling skills and suggested I speak with her about my experience. I met her and shared a couple of the stories and she agreed to meet with me. I thanked her as she walked me to the door, she quietly asked, "Who is helping you?" I repeated the question, "Who's helping me?" I was a little taken aback. No one *ever* in my life asked me that question. I was taught to take care of myself and don't complain. Handle it. I looked at her and knew the question was sincere. She repeated herself and said, you are suffering a loss too. I was silent. To be totally honest, I didn't want to feel. I just wanted to do something to make it better. A quick fix. Arnell reached out to me the next week and we had our first session at a local coffee shop. She didn't know me and I didn't know her; however, she took the time to listen, and shared with me that God is in control. He is almighty and he loves me. I didn't realize how much I needed "*her*", someone who didn't know me, didn't judge me, didn't interrupt my sentences, and didn't tell me "*her*" stories, as a remedy to heal my hurt and pain. She listened. Yes, just listened! I *felt* she understood and genuinely cared about (me) *Shirley*. And I finally cried. I thank God for allowing our paths to cross. A year later, I wanted to form a prayer group of educators focused on spiritual support in our profession. I asked Arnell to assist me and of course, she agreed. Within our power group of 10 women, Arnell did way more than assist. She lead, served, and supported and continues to do so. She always brings light and positivity into the conversation but doesn't hesitate to "*keep it real*" when needed. Arnell Evans shares her life stories in order to provide honesty and realness to her world. She uses her trials, victories, and happy moments as tools to help others see "a" way when they were convinced there wasn't one. She remains a "checker upper" and has become a central body to our prayer call *and* to all whom she comes in contact.

The day I met Arnell – she was in full bloom. God allowed the storms in her life; for they created strength and determination in her walk. The Lord chose her to be a catalyst for inspirational change. Yes, she dealt with a plethora of situations and circumstances; however, he gave her the tenacity to get through the storms to become the beautiful flower who has blossomed into a dedicated servant of our God. Each and every day touching those that He allows to cross her path. Continuing to say yes and making a difference in the lives of those she touches. Thank you Arnell Evans for being obedient and for teaching me that it is ok to cry. Joy will come in the morning. The sun will shine again and I "to" will blossom. Thank you Arnell! Your sister in Christ, Shirley Dr. Shirley Rose-Gilliam is a 34-year veteran educator. *Her experiences as a child have been both a catalyst for changing her situation and today motivates her to answer the special "calling" to make a difference in the lives of youth. She has made her greatest impact as a mentor, coach, and thought partner to educators at all levels. She currently serves as an advocate for education in her community as the Vice-President of the Fort Bend ISD Board of Trustees, in Sugar Land, Texas.*

INTRODUCTION

This book weaves the art of giving flowers with the power of spoken word and affirmation, illuminating a path from despair to empowerment. Drawing from biblical references and the creative potential of language, this journey is a testament to the blossoming that occurs when we infuse our lives with the beauty of giving. In short, this book is a message of hope, to the emotional deprived child, adolescent, teen, teen mom, single mom, recovering alcoholic, cocaine addict, debtor, codependent, compulsive overeater, adult child of an alcoholic, a recovering Christian, married mom with a blended family, and many others…. but God has delivered me out of them all (My God is masculine).

It is my desire to inspire you to explore your own journey – past, present and future with hope as well as to see how my story can reflect their story and see how it is a gift of flowers to me.

Welcome to the Journey!

THE POWER OF OUR SPOKEN WORD

Amplified and King James Version of the Bible

God Spoke the Word

In the beginning, there was nothing but a vast, empty area. Then, with a single command, God spoke into the darkness, saying, "Let there be light!" And instantly, light bursts forth, filling the universe with its brilliant light. This was the remarkable beginning of all creation, as told in Genesis 1:1 and 1:3 NIV

God Wrote the Word

And he wrote on the tables, according to the first writing, the ten commandments, which the Lord spoke unto you. Deuteronomy 10:4, 4:13 NIV

In God's divine wisdom, He inscribed the very words of morality and guidance onto stone tablets. These words were none other than the sacred Ten Commandments, delivered by the Lord Himself, as recounted in Deuteronomy 10:4 and 4:13. This act marked the beginning of what would guide the hearts and actions of humanity for generations.

All Scripture is given by inspiration of God, and is profitable for doctrine, for reproof, for correction, for instruction in righteousness, that the man of God may be complete, thoroughly equipped for every good work. 2 Timothy 3:16-17 NIV

As revealed in 2 Timothy 3:16-17, all scripture, including those commandments carved in stone, is a gift from God, inspired by His divine wisdom. It serves as a fountain of knowledge and morality, providing guidance for doctrine, correction, and righteousness. Through these sacred words, the path to wholeness and the tools for honorable living are bestowed upon the faithful, ensuring they are equipped for every good work in life.

God then Revealed the Word in Human Form

In the beginning was the Word, and the Word was with God, and the Word was God Himself. John 1:1 NIV

And the Word was made Flesh and made His dwelling among us, and we beheld His glory. John 1:14 NIV

Man shall not live by bread alone; but man lives by every word that proceeds from the mouth of the Lord. Deuteronomy 8:3b NIV

And Jesus said to them, "I am the bread of life. He who comes to Me shall never hunger, and he who believes in Me shall never thirst. John 6:35 NIV

In the beginning, there existed a Word. This Word, it's said, wasn't just any ordinary word; it was divine, and it was with God. In fact, it was God Himself. This concept is captured in the verse from John 1:1 NIV

This Word, which was divine and with God, took on a human form. It became flesh and dwelled among us, as John 1:14 NIV recounts.

As found in Deuteronomy 8:3b., it was declared that life isn't sustained solely by bread but by every word that flows from the mouth of the Lord,

Jesus Himself declared, "I am the bread of life. Those who come to Me will never go hungry, and those who believe in Me will never thirst." This proclamation, recorded in John 6:35, conveyed the idea that Jesus embodied not just food for the body, but for the soul as well, and that one could find the fulfillment of their spiritual hunger and thirst by coming to Him and believing in Him.

Made in God's Image and Likeness

We are crafted in the image and likeness of God, as we engage in speech, writing, and artistic expression, our words possess the profound ability to heal wounds, inspire, and either breathe life or cause harm. Our words are powerful beyond what we can imagine.

***Seeds for Meditation:* What does the power of God's word mean to you?**

Back in the day, the guiding principles for living right focused on being kind to others and the importance of sharing with one another. We were instilled with the wisdom that if we couldn't find something kind to say about someone, it was better to remain silent. These were indeed valuable principles to live by, as highlighted in the passage from "Every day is Mother's Day."

In Proverbs 16:24 NIV, we find the timeless wisdom that gracious words resemble a honeycomb, offering sweetness to the soul and promoting healing within the very core of our being. Our words are powerful beyond what we can imagine.

***Seeds for Meditation:* How did the word of God influence your life growing up?**

BIOGRAPHY

Mrs. Arnell Evans, a Licensed Chemical Dependency Counselor and Certified Anger Resolution Therapist and formerly a Peer Recovery Support Specialist. Ms. Evans has worked for over 20 years in the fields of substance abuse counseling and co-dependency. She specializes in working with women, adolescents, and groups.

In addition to Licensed Chemical Dependency Counseling practices and procedures, Mrs. Evans interacts with clients and all licensed professionals in the field. She possesses the skills and the talent to offer counseling in a fun, interactive and engaging manner which appeals to teens. Through her innovative counseling practices, she assists teens to develop new coping strategies and leadership skills. In turn, these tools empower teens to navigate their daily lives and to overcome their inevitable challenges. Her experience skills and talents continue to empower women to be the best they can be and to give their gifts and talents to their families and community through healing of childhood traumas.

Mrs. Evans served as Program Manager for TAFS, an adolescent peer group organization, 4 years and worked with students as substance use disorder (SUDS) Counselor at a local charter school and one of the local churches in the area. At the charter school Ms. Evans served as a referral and substance misuse, mental health counselor,4 years, located in the heart of an area which was known as the 3rd most dangerous community in the country, according to a recent study. Currently, DWI/

DUI counselor. She grew up in a single parent home and also by her grandparents when the Third Ward and Sunnyside community was safe to reside. In substance misuse recovery for over 25 years, she is keenly aware of the lack of recovery resources available to inner city adolescents and how critical having access to good recovery programs is to youth and their families. Mrs. Evans has made it her mission to bring critical resources and peer recovery initiatives to a neighborhood voted as one of the toughest in the nation. Ms. Evans, also served as a Speaker for the Generation Found Film Documentary, which premieres across the world in September 2016 in selected theatres and soon on Netflix and Amazon. Mr. & Mrs. Evans are an integral part of the film which specifies the lack of recovery resources in the inner-city areas of Houston, and surrounding areas. Mrs. Evans is active in her church and has facilitated Bible study classes in churches in her neighborhood for over 15 years. Is active in numerous 12 Step programs to continue her healing and to help others become free from addictions and compulsions.

Establishing trust plays a critical role when introducing new programs to inner city neighborhoods and powerful change occurs when transformation comes from within the community itself. Married for 23 years with five children and four grandchildren at the writing of this book, now a GG (great grand mom to a beautiful boy King). Mrs. Evans is an example for and trusted advocate of inner-city families who have been affected by the devastation of drugs and alcohol and have the desire to be healthy by staying clean and sober. *"An addiction is an emergency when it becomes that individual's crisis"* is a quote that provides her with daily inspiration.

One of my cherished past times is indulging in a bit of retail therapy, finding joy in the fascination of shoes, furniture, and fine art. I have an insatiable appetite for knowledge, diving into inspirational books, videos, autobiographies, and documentaries that enrich my perception of the world.

I find great satisfaction in sharing motivational speeches, especially with young adults and individuals from all walks of life. It's a way for me to give back and be of service. I believe in and inspired by Shirley Chisholm's wisdom, "service is the rent we pay for living on this Earth."

(I draw inspiration from the wisdom of those who have come

before us, particularly the powerful statement by Shirley Chisolm that "service is the rent we pay for living on this Earth." This quote resonates deeply with my belief in the importance of giving back and making a meaningful impact in our world.)

When it comes to leisure and relaxation, I seek comfort in watching movies and exploring new destinations. Among my favorite vacation spots are Jamaica, the Bahamas, New York, Catalina Island, Paris, and Lahaina, Hawaii. Though I haven't yet set foot in the Holy Land, I hold onto the hope that, God willing, I will have the opportunity to visit soon.

For over 15 years, I've dedicated myself to working with single women, nurturing their self-acceptance and self-awareness, and providing hope as they make life's choices. I've also extended my hand to children who society has labeled "at-risk" in school. I believe every individual deserves a chance to thrive. I believe the only way to keep what I have; I must give it away. Doing what you really love to do is a great experience that I wish everyone could have. I've come to understand that success hinges on authenticity and integrity. I've learned not to fear mistakes or the judgment of others. If there's something you aspire to do, don't hesitate to pursue it.

A great piece of wisdom I have learned is to stop trying to look good to avoid looking bad, everyone makes mistakes in life and at work. If there's something you want to do, don't be afraid to do it!

I reflect upon the words of my three adolescent children who, in their own unique way, have been part of my transformation. Their support and pride in my journey remind me of the grace of God that filled the void within me, *"Mom we are so glad you got your life together, because we don't know what we would have done or where we would be; probably with at least 3 kids and on monthly state welfare!"* But for the grace of God, I am so glad God filled the hole inside and now, I have the privilege of inspiring countless children, just as they continue to inspire me every day.

CHAPTER 1

The Power of the Spoken Word and the Gift of Flowers – Adolescent Years

Step into the realm of words and blossoms, discovering their profound impact. This chapter uncovers the significance of the spoken word through biblical context and the concept of creation. Just as spoken words shape reality, so do the petals of flowers unfold into life's vibrant tapestry, inspiring us to embrace transformation.

My life lessons along with the abundant blessings of God

My passions encompass two deeply meaningful areas of focus. Firstly, I am driven to help children who have felt neglected during their formative years, extending a helping hand to nurture their well-being and offer them the care and attention they deserve. Additionally, my commitment extends to aiding underserved women and children, along with their families, who have been impacted by the challenges posed by drugs and alcohol. In these two realms, I find purpose and fulfillment in making a positive difference in the lives of those who need it most.

I belong to the Baby Boomer generation, and my birthdate coincides with April 20th, the same day as National Smoke Out Day. Throughout my life, I've seen this date as particularly unique and meaningful. Surprisingly, it's only recently that I've started to view myself in a similar special light. I was born on an Easter Sunday to my 24-year-old mother and 18-year-old father, they never married (she playfully called herself the OG Cougar).

At that time, I had three sisters and one brother. My mother had difficulty during my birth - she almost died - so they had to do some type of surgery so that she could live, and she bears the scar on her arm as a reminder. I believed this caused me to experience fetal distress in the womb. My mother had been married and divorced in her early 20's and I felt my arrival was not at a good time in her life. I was my father's first child. He had just finished high school but with a child on the way he had to decide what he needed to do to take care of a family. My father and mother were cohabitating or "shacking up" during a time when society thought it was without morals and values. Prior to the 1970s, having a child out of wedlock carried a stigma, and in those days, someone without an education or a stable job often found themselves unjustly labeled as a 'low life' or 'loser.' My mother always had a job as a cook. My father, however, defied those stereotypes. He always had at least one job, sometimes even two, to assist his parents. But when times grew tougher, with the responsibility of caring for a little girl, he realized he needed to marry the woman he loved. Unfortunately, things didn't go as they desired.

My mother, who had a prior marriage and four children of her own, it seemed as though she was viewed as 'unsuitable' by my paternal grandmother, who also happened to be a Pastor's wife. She seemed to strongly opposed their union; concerned about her son's promising future. In response, my father made a significant decision. He enlisted in the U.S. Army and then the U.S. Air Force, seeking skills and security that would pave the way for a successful career once his service was complete.

Our caretakers, be it parents or guardians, played significant roles in shaping our early lives. Reflecting on the past, I've come to realize that my mother, driven by her fears and sometimes influenced by libations, would occasionally assume the role of an authoritarian figure, displaying moments of anger and making demands. In her world, she was infallible, and her words were law. We, the children, were conditioned to be seen and not heard, with our emotional needs largely unmet—no hugs, no words of love.

***Seeds for Meditation:* What's your present-day relationship with the "childhood memory" of your mother, father, or caretaker?**

My father had drifted out of my daily existence, only returning for fleeting moments during his two-week furlough. I distinctly remember a moment when I was just four years old, meeting his family for the first time. They knew of my existence, but I remained oblivious to their presence.

In those times, my mother was the maestro of emotional and mental torment. She had a knack for ensuring you never forgot your wrongdoings, a skill she shared with my aunt and other family members. It felt like they were always ready to dredge up past mistakes, no matter how much effort I put into changing my life.

It seemed the adults in our lives were more inclined to scorn than to offer praise or encouragement. Perhaps it reflected the hardships they endured during those trying times, a way of preparing us for the inevitable challenges that lie ahead. We were raised mostly by our grandparents, my mother's parents who gave us a decent life and always reminded us that education and hard work was important.

My father's duty in the armed forces took him away frequently, leaving me emotionally and physically distant from him. However, I held a special place in his heart, and I was his cherished princess. When I was ten years old, he married, and it felt as if my sense of security had been torn apart. His new wife came into our lives with her three children.

Regrettably, it felt like my stepmother harbored jealousy toward the bond I shared with my father, and I felt unwelcome. While her mistreatment of me was not physical, it was a form of emotional disappointment that left deep scars. I couldn't help but ponder whether she might have considered less desirable actions, as she did with her own children, if she believed she could escape consequences.

While growing up, it often felt like I was constantly in trouble, as if I were somehow unlikable to those around me. My mother had her share of boyfriends and went on to have three more children. Eventually, she got married again, and this time she married my two younger siblings' father; a man I couldn't shake the feeling that he didn't care for me. I felt he held some resentment; because he felt the guys I dated was not suited for me. (I must admit, he was right)

In this complex family dynamic, I also had an aunt who displayed unkindness toward me, except for one of my siblings who was two years older. My sibling was raised by my aunt, leaving the rest of us feeling the weight of her unkindness. My aunt appeared to be very lonely and bitter.

During those years, a sense of being lost and alone hung heavily over me. My sibling stepped into the role of a surrogate parent after our Dad left for military service. However, when my sibling graduated from high school, he decided to follow in my Dad's footsteps and join the Air Force, often mentioning that my Dad had been a mentor to him, seemingly because his relationship with his biological father was sometimes rocky. But even their father treated us as if we were his own children. This sense of belonging was incredibly comforting for a young girl like me. I distinctly recall how their father always made me feel as if I were truly his own. Amid it all, my father would later say that I had essentially raised myself, because my Mom was rarely there; her work and her social life kept her away a lot.

In those formative years, I became an avid reader, immersing myself in books as a way to stay out of the way and avoid being scolded or hurt emotionally. Our living situation often involved being with our maternal grandparents, where television time was restricted, ending promptly at 8:00pm. As a result, we turned to the radio and crafted our own imaginative games to fill the void. And yes, we learned the art of playing cards, even though it was frowned upon.

Our world was further constrained by the rule that we could only play with children whose parents were known to our grandparents or those who appeared 'neat' and 'educated.' Card games were strictly off-limits, it was seen as "gambling" my grandparents would say.

In response to these limitations, we were instilled with a strong work ethic and a commitment to getting a good education. We learned how to maintain a household, pick figs from the fig tree, and crush grapes for my grandfather's wine-making endeavors. Additionally, my siblings and cousins would join the men of our family on Friday fishing trips. Our extended family included educators, renowned musicians, talented cooks, and entrepreneurs, shaping us with a rich tapestry of skills and influences.

Our grandparents' retirement story was as unique as it was inspiring. They had their apartments, nestled on the same property behind their home—a labor of love built by my grandfather and his friends, toiling away after their demanding day jobs in the meat packing industry. The tale he shared with us was a testament to their unwavering dedication and tireless efforts to secure their retirement.

I've always held onto this memory as a reminder that the entrepreneurial spirit and determination ran deep in our family's DNA. If they could carve out a stable financial future, then I knew that same tenacity flowed within me, connecting me to the resilience of my ancestors.

My father's parents embodied strictness, were reserved and had a strong religious commitment (although my father's church attendance dwindled after turning 18). Whenever my dad would take me to their house, I'd often arrive disheveled, bearing the traces of dirt and an unpleasant odor, accompanied by a suitcase filled with soiled clothes. It was under their guidance that I learned the importance of cleanliness, as they patiently taught me how to take care of myself. They even began providing me with clean clothes and underwear for our church visits.

I can still hear my grandmother's words echoing in my ears: "You go in there and take a number 5 bath." It was her way of saying I needed to bathe five times until I was not just clean but smelled good too! Our Sundays were filled with three church services, and we faithfully attended on Wednesdays and Fridays as well. If there was a church revival happening, whether it was summer, winter, or spring or fall, we were there every single night.

During my adolescence, I yearned for an escape. I held onto the hope of finding my knight in shining armor, believing that any boy who showed me attention might be the one to rescue me. In my daydreams, I envisioned a life where we'd build a family filled with love, and we'd live out our happily ever after together.

I got pregnant at 14 and had my first child - a girl - at age 15. I was seen as the one who brought shame to both sides of my family. Once again, I felt lost and alone. It seemed that no one shared in my happiness or celebrated my joys. As a matter of fact, my grandmother on my father's side wanted me to give up my child but my mother would want nothing of it but instead was willing to accept seeking adoption. It felt like my dad had no say in the matter, at the time, my stepmother was expecting my little brother. My father would then have three children with her to take care of. I felt unwanted and disliked by everyone in my family, even by God.

My sole intention was to transition into adulthood, hoping to remove myself from everyone's path so they could lead their lives without my presence as a burden. I repeatedly vowed never to follow in my mother's footsteps, yet I found myself mirroring her in ways I had vowed to avoid.

My next ten years were a terrible time in my life. I was making all the wrong decisions. I was into underage drinking, promiscuity and smoking marijuana at age 18, and by then, I had my son. I only remember three feelings all my life: fear, loneliness, and anger. I was in a physically, mentally, and emotionally unhealthy relationship for 10 years (I have vivid memories of my mother and stepfather engaging in nightly disputes, characterized by his verbal threats, yet he never resorted to physical harm.). It seemed to me like I was repeating the cycle!

I started getting involved in more relationships that were either physically, emotionally, or mentally unhealthy for me. I found myself trapped in this relentless cycle, mirroring my mother's actions. I later understood in therapy that I recreating my childhood trauma because that was all I knew. Then I welcomed my third and fourth babies into the world—two beautiful daughters—by men who were cruel and lacked commitment. One day, I promised myself I would not engage in an unhealthy relationship. I kept my promise, and as a result, I started feeling a glimmer of strength and a hint of self-love. It was just a small amount, but it was sufficient enough to catapult me into a state of awareness where I felt ready to seek help from God.

"Family Rules: 'Don't talk, don't trust, don't feel" book ...is a line spoken by all who have been raised in a family where one or both parents could have a problem with some sort of dependence...it could also include other disorders. Excerpt taken from," It Will Never Happen To Me" book by Claudia Black

Flowers of Reflection:

What are some mistakes you made in your childhood and young adult life? Have you accepted your past mistakes? For example, things you have done or said. Words can blossom into reality. Have you discovered their profound impact on your life?

Petal Playbook – Time For Action:

1. Acknowledge your past mistakes
2. Learn from your past so that you can heal
3. Practice self-compassion, and forgiveness for yourself
4. Ask your "tribe" to offer affirmations that can be healing from the early season of your life

Words of Comfort: **The Lord is my shepherd; I have everything I need (Psalm 23:1 GNT).**

CHAPTER 2

Portrait of Resilience: The Early Years

In this chapter, we delve into Arnell's childhood – her early fears and experiences and will to overcome circumstances that surrounded her. It is here that the art of giving flowers takes root as a symbol of compassion and connection.

When a Child is suffering from mistreatment in the home and misuse of controlled substances, their growth and development is greatly affected, and he or she can become stagnant.

Adolescence Days of Dreams and Nightmares

I remember my childhood was full of fear, terror and pain. My earliest recollection takes me back to when I was just four years old, a time when I had to venture beyond the comforting and secure walls of my grandmother's home. There, amidst the company of caring adults and the freedom of play, I reveled in undivided attention and the joy of doing as I pleased.

However, the day arrived when I had to step into the world of nursery school (PreK). I was engulfed by fear and reluctance to leave behind the cozy haven of my grandmother's house, where I felt cherished and could indulge in playtime as I wished.

The challenge arose as I had to learn how to "fit in" with the other children at the day school who appeared to navigate this new environment with ease. I experienced a sense of abandonment when my mother occasionally arrived late, or when my father dropped me off. It was even more disheartening when the lady driving the station wagon, brimming with kids, would pick me up and seat me at the far back, facing the window. She would transport me to a church where the school for four-year-olds was held. I had grown accustomed to the simple pleasure of my grandmamma's sandwiches, made with bread, butter, and sugar—oh, the sweetness of that sugar! However, as I began to mature, I realized that I, too, had to adapt, just like the other children. The days of having things my way was fading, and I no longer had the freedom to play alone with my imaginary friends until naptime. Instead, my lunch kit now held only those bread, butter, and sugar sandwiches, to be savored during lunchtime at school.

It was during this time that I encountered my first real-life giants—my uncles, my father's brothers. I also had the opportunity to meet my father's side of the family for the first time. Their excitement to see me was palpable, but once again, I was filled with fear. I was the first "little one" to grace their household, and as a result, I became the center of their attention.

As far back as I can remember, I harbored a deep fear of the dark and anything that covered my head; it terrified me. Nightmares plagued my sleep each and every night. I would desperately try to ward off these monsters, attempting to pray them away and wishing them gone by repeating phrases like "star light, star bright" or "now I lay me down to sleep." But despite my efforts, the monsters would always return once the lights were extinguished, robbing me of a peaceful rest and leaving me exhausted for school the next morning. There were days that I would just daydream because I was so sleepy.

Interestingly, I discovered a means to contend with those nightmares when I was at my grandmamas and granddaddies, as I affectionately called my mother's parents. For my father's parents, I had a different set of names: Big Mama and Big Daddy.

At grandmama's house, she kindly left the bathroom light on for me until I drifted into slumber, which provided me with immense comfort. However, this arrangement did not sit well with my sisters, who grew increasingly agitated because they couldn't sleep with the light on, leading to their own disruptions. Unfortunately, this meant that after a while, I would invariably awaken from a nightmare, finding myself shrouded in total darkness, a circumstance that intensified my fear.

***Seeds of Meditation:* What were your childhood insecurities or fears that were not acknowledged? How did this affect the way you responded to life?**

Big Mama, Big Daddy, and even the giants in the house, along with my aunts, remained unaware of my nightly nightmares. However, one weekend while staying with them, I experienced a particularly terrifying nightmare that left me screaming and crying, convinced that something was lurking in the chair, fixated on me.

They reassured me that nothing was amiss, that there was nothing in the house. But I insisted, pointing, and saying, "There it is! Right there!" To quell my fears, they switched on the lights, only to reveal that the source of my terror was a stuffed animal—a wolf they had bought for me. They attempted to convince me of its harmlessness. Despite this incident, they too began leaving the lights on until I could drift into slumber, a routine they adopted for many nights. However, my aunts, much like my sisters, expressed frustration at the notion of sleeping with the lights on, a sentiment I never quite comprehended.

Again, I started saying my prayers asking God to take away the bad dreams and the monsters, but to no avail.

Whenever I stayed with my mother, she would not keep the light on for me until I went to sleep; instead, she would make me sit in the bathroom all night until I fell asleep on the toilet seat until morning, boy did my neck hurt!

All the religious adults (my dad's side) said, "it's the devil that she is so bad!" my family would laugh and tease me. Every single day, my siblings would taunt me, poking fun at my fear of imaginary monsters that only I seemed to see. They would laugh and ridicule me, urging me to leave. All I yearned for was to be close to them and to feel like I belonged.

Using hurtful words and harsh verbal remarks can leave deep

emotional scars on a child that stick with them for a long time. These scars can make them feel less confident and good about

themselves. It can also affect how they do in school, work, and with friends. It's even been shown to cause mental health problems and change how their brain works (adapted from "The Hurtful Words Adults Use That Harm Children The Most" by Natasha Hinde)

"Words carry so much power with children – we all need to build them up, not knock them down." - Natasha Hinde

Flowers of Reflection:

Have you forgiven your Caretakers for the harmful words they spoke to you? Have you forgiven yourself and others for their mistakes?

Petal Playbook – Time For Action:

I affirm that I forgive ______________

*I affirm that I forgive*______________

*I affirm that I forgive*______________

Words of Comfort: **Who forgives all your sins, Who heals all your diseases (dis-eases) emphasis added. Psalms 103:3 NIV**

CHAPTER 3

From Darkness to Light: Overcoming Adversity

This chapter highlights how Arnell navigates her struggles—identity crises, family dynamics, and her battle with despair. The loss of a child becomes a pivotal moment that propels her towards spiritual growth. As flowers break through the soil towards the sun, so does Arnell's journey ascend from darkness to the radiant light of faith and empowerment.

Fights for my life as Teenager/Young Adult

I know that our parents, caretakers, did the best they could in raising us and helping us to grow and develop as babies, children, adolescents, and young adults.

As I was growing up as an adolescent and teenager, I never thought life could be any different than it was. I can vividly remember my time in 8th grade at Ryan Junior High School. Those were the days of attending football games, forging new friendships, and feeling that burgeoning interest in boys, fueled by the longing for love. It was during this time that I encountered a young man who harbored strong feelings for me. On one of the many occasions, we spent together, the unexpected happened – my first daughter was conceived - who came into the world on October 11, 1972. We named her "Lakeshia Renee", part of her dad's middle name and my middle name. But we called her "Cricket" as an endearing nickname she was so cute and small like a little cricket! It felt as though that moment marked the onset of chaos, confusion, pain and fear; a time when I seemed to lose control of my life and my sense of self. I could feel some of my family members detach and distanced themselves from me because I was a disgrace to them by getting pregnant at age 14 and becoming a mother at 15.

Seeds of Meditation: What adversities did you encounter growing up and as a young adult?

Starting my own family

As I grieved the loss of my first child "Cricket" a precious and beautiful 3-year-old angel, on April 16, 1976, which fell on Good Friday, my heart ached. Just two days later, on Sunday, April 18, 1976, Easter Sunday, and then again on Monday, April 19, 1976, we held wake services to honor my child's memory. Amidst the somberness of those days, there was a glimmer of hope as my 11-month-old son, Derrick, took his first steps on Monday, April 19 the night of her viewing and her service on Tuesday, April 20, 1976. It was a bittersweet moment, as it coincided with the day of my child's funeral services, a day that was meant to be a celebration of my 19th birthday. So, while I marked another year of life, I also bid farewell to my firstborn.

This wasn't how it was meant to be. Children were supposed to bid farewell to their parents, not the other way around. It wasn't part of God's original plan. What happened? My mind struggled to comprehend how, in a single moment, she had been there one day and gone the next, vanishing so swiftly. It was a tragic reality that I would have to carry with me for the rest of my life, a deep void etched into my heart and existence.

I questioned how I would navigate each passing day, how I would cope with this overwhelming grief. At that moment, I found myself thinking that if this was what life had in store, I didn't want it. And with that, my life began a downward spiral. During those days, I had no knowledge of clinical depression, and my family lacked the understanding of such matters. Back then, it wasn't even called that.

***Seeds of Meditation:* Have you ever felt or experienced abandonment, emotionally or physically? If so, how did you overcome to feel safe emotionally and physically?**

All the teens and young adults in the neighborhood thought that my mom and siblings were the coolest in town because they could do things that other kids couldn't do in her presence.

To ease the pain and to relieve the depression, I was prescribed medication for the trauma which caused a dependence because of prolonged use, and later introduced to alcohol and illegal substances.

***Seeds of Meditation:* What was traumatic for you as a child, teen, young adult? people, places, events, beliefs or anything.**

I was estranged from my family, and I was really angry and my mom and my dad for a very long time. Today, they are my biggest champions of support. I recall how my mom gave up her job to take care of my kids after her husband died. We had an agreement that I could pay her as she kept my kids so that I could finish school and go to college and get a better job and maybe a career. But my addiction did not let me; Despite countless failed relationships, the web of lies, and the heartaches of disappointment, my mom was my constant companion until I slipped into a darker hole and became dependent on more substances. My mom and siblings were not aware; they could go out and have fun drinking sociably, but I needed more to cover my pain from the death of my daughter and the unwholesome relationships I kept secret. I was definitely on a suicide mission and so, it became a self-fulfilling prophecy, echoing the sentiment I had once uttered: "If this is life, I do not want it."

I kept asking myself repeatedly, "Why did my little girl (Cricket) have to die?"

After near death experiences and embarking on a series of reckless actions that could have led me to incarceration, pitiful and incomprehensive demoralization (P.A.I.D.) (from Alcoholics Anonymous) I paid a high cost! I finally hit my rock bottom and thank God I did!

At the beginning of the end of my ordeal, my kids and I moved in with my dad. I felt secure again just like that "little girl" My dad had divorced his first wife and he said I could come and stay with him to get my life on track. I knew he meant business, so I was able to enter a treatment program to get help.

The impact of my decisions

My regrets are that I neglected my children and robbed them of emotional attachment. I could not nurture them because I was afraid that if I loved them as much as I loved "Cricket", my first born I would lose them too! One day, my daughter (one of my miracle chocolate pies, God blessed me with another little girl) asked, "why did you not take us with you when you would leave in a car?" (this was a 1 year into my recovery) I had another moment of clarity; I did not realize that's what was happening, (sometimes it was because I was going away for some days to party and get high) but realized I was afraid I could not protect them from hurt or harm if something happened. Then my AA sponsor would encourage me to start with baby steps and to trust God. We then started taking vacations where we would be in the car together! Look at God!

Years later, I felt a longing to visit with the family that took care of me and allowed me to live with them and they took care of Cricket, my first born for the three years that she lived. It was her biological father and his parents. Since I had not really sat down and talked to them since the day of the car accident years prior, I was nervous and deeply emotional. I had to get to another place spiritually and not stuff the painful feelings any longer. I prayed for the courage to visit. I asked myself "what if they do not want to see me?" Before this time, I saw them in a shopping mall and introduced them to my husband. I did see them about 5 years prior during one of my drugging escapades.

So, this had to be the day to do the visit; I shared it in the AA meeting after being called on by surprise, I really did not want to let others know. But once again the principles of the AA program kicked in and "God did for me what I could not do for myself." So, I shared my fears with the group and shed a lot of tears. Right after the meeting, I felt some level of courage and I jumped in my car and headed for "Cricket's" grandparents' house at last!

I prayed the serenity prayer because I was very nervous however, I arrived feeling some peace and calm, I knocked on the door and finally someone came; it was a beautiful young lady, she said "hello, and I said, "Is the lady of the house in?" and she said just a minute." She came back after it seem like a long time and said" who are you?" I said, "my name is Arnell." She went back and stayed for a very long time; my mind said, "what if she does not want to see me, what if she say, "tell her I am not here?" I did not know what was going on, so I started to get afraid again, and I thought about leaving. I said, "well at least I tried" But I stayed at the door and then the door opened and to my surprise the door opens widely and there she was My daughter Cricket's grandmother, looking the same! She grabbed me and I grabbed her with a flood gate of tears. She hugged me ever so tightly and I held her tightly, too. I cried and she said, "it's ok; How are You?" I said through my tears, "not so good, I have been trying to get here for years but I could not make it because of my fears." She invited me to come in and sit down, she said, "Freddie is in Pennsylvania, I will call him and tell him you are here!" He and I spoked briefly; it had been a long time since I spoke to him or saw him. (he has took sick and passed, during the writing of this book)

Flowers of reflection:

How have you overcome adversity? What are some of your obstacles and fears? How can you sow some seeds of change?

Petal Playbook – Time for Action:

"Feel the fear and do it anyway!" Susan Jeffers, *Author, Feel the Fear and Do it Anyway*

1. Identify and acknowledge the fear.
2. Break it down into small steps.
3. Be positive and visualize yourself overcoming.

Words of Comfort: **The Lord is my light and my salvation— whom shall, I fear? The LORD is the stronghold of my life— of whom shall I be afraid? Psalm 27:1 NIV**

CHAPTER 4

Cultivating Belief, Nurturing Vision

Trace Arnell's transformation as she shifts from "I can't" to "I can." This chapter delves into her evolving beliefs, shaping her vision for change. The art of giving flowers weaves its way through her desire to support underserved youth and families, blooming as a symbol of hope and renewal.

In my beliefs, I find a profound and transformative journey, one marked by faith, resilience, and self-discovery. I embrace the presence of a higher power, recognizing that there is a divine force greater than myself. I am a Christian, rooted in the Trinity of God the Father, God the Son, and God the Holy Spirit.

My convictions extend beyond spirituality. They encompass everything about my life – work, relationships, money, life, and most importantly, myself. Through my trials and triumphs, I've learned that the past does not define me; rather, it propels me toward a future filled with growth, redemption, and boundless possibilities. My faith in a higher power, coupled with a deep belief in my own capacity for change, fuels my journey toward a brighter, purpose-filled life.

Beliefs

In the AA program's wisdom, it proclaims, "God is either everything or He is nothing," and in my heart, my Higher Power is masculine. I hold firm in my belief in the existence of God, recognizing that I am not God; I am merely a humble soul and to me, God is everything. As a Christian, my faith centers on the Trinity—God the Father, God the Son, and God the Holy Spirit. This triune presence guides my spiritual journey.

Work

In the past, my belief was shackled by doubt—I thought, "I can't," in many areas of my life because I hadn't completed my basic education; I dropped out during the 11th grade. The reasons were simple: I had three children, no marketable skills, and no job prospects.

But then, a pivotal moment arrived. I found the courage and decided to apply for college, a daring step forward. Yet, I faced another hurdle—I needed my GED. To assess my eligibility for a grant-funded class, I took an aptitude test. Surprisingly, my score soared to impressive heights. The administrator, acknowledging this, chose not to pay for the class. Instead, they provided me with a GED book and instructed me to study diligently for 30 days before taking the exam. I complied, and at the age of around 24, I passed the GED! I felt that finally things were looking up for me.

Another instance involved a lie detector test during a job application process at a bank, a savings and loan institution. The officer conducting the test asked what was on my mind when a particular question arose. I honestly responded that I wasn't thinking; I was singing a song in my head. He probed further, asking which song it was. I told him, "The Lord is blessing me right now!" Remarkably, I passed the test.

These experiences marked the beginning of my belief in myself. Others recognized my potential and offered affirmations. My perspective about my life shifted in a positive direction.

Love

In the past, my journey through love and relationships was marked by darkness—a state of abuse that touched every facet of my being, be it physical, mental, emotional, spiritual, or financial. I was trapped in a paradox, attempting to embody an adult's responsibilities within the confines of a child's body and mind. Unconsciously, I expected the guys in my life to exhibit the qualities of men, a burden they were not equipped to bear.

***Seeds of Meditation:* "What habits, whether they are conscious or unconscious, that have supported your sense of safety and love as you've entered young adulthood?"**

Today, my path towards healing necessitates a crucial step—looking back at my past to pave the way forward. It's about excavating, exploring, and ultimately shedding the layers of my old notions and childish beliefs, not just about myself but also about my parents and all types of relationships in my life. Importantly, I've learned not to assign blame to my parents for the choices I made. Instead, I delve into my past to gain insight into myself and to release its hold on my present and future. It is a journey worth taking.

Money

My relationship with money was once shrouded in ignorance—I had no understanding of how to save or manage it. In my family, conversations about bills and debt were laden with anxiety, as if they were burdens too heavy to bear. This left me in a state of confusion, struggling with financial concepts I couldn't grasp.

Interestingly, my father had knowledge of managing money, thanks to his service in the military, and he maintained an excellent credit record. However, he did not pass those lessons on to me.

During the early stages of my recovery, I decided to join Debtors Anonymous. This marked a turning point in my financial journey. Through this organization, I began to adopt a new mindset about how to handle money wisely. It was through this transformation that I achieved a significant milestone—I purchased my first home with an astonishingly low closing cost was minimum, what a blessing! Such a feat was unheard of in the mortgage world, but I knew that it was a testament to the power of faith and the effectiveness of the 12-step program that had already worked wonders in my battle against my substance misuse.

This newfound faith gave me the confidence that I could also attain financial wealth, even though I had amassed a substantial amount of debt during my addiction while striving to provide for my three children as a single mother.

Life Challenges

Today, my life stands as a testament to my journey—a journey of redemption, growth, and an unwavering belief that, no matter the challenges, I am the author of my own narrative, and I hold the pen to script a future filled with purpose and possibility.

During the year of Hurricane Rita and Katrina, my daughter married a man whose nature was telling in his temperament and that relationship did not work out. They separated and he chose to take their daughter out of the country; she was only a year and a half. That resonated with me because often people seek out what they know and that's how they end up in some relationships. At the time, from my own life, I understood that mental or social disorders are generally unhealthy and can be seen as excessive in a given individual to the point, they cause harm or severe disruption to their lifestyle.

I saw myself in my daughter because I recognized, through this relationship, she recreated the dynamics of her childhood, without knowing it (Selah).

***Seeds of Meditation:* Which habits that you carried into adulthood have been sources of discomfort, pain, or challenges for you?**

We went through a lot of mental and emotional pain; feelings of lost, hopelessness and feelings of failure. It felt as though some days I would not make it. The family was under a lot of duress and my heart was so heavy. The pain was great as if I was re-living the trauma of my loss and past relationships. My husband would come home from work not understanding how to console his wife and daughter.

During that time, I was strong in my faith, and in my relationship with God. I was an Armor-of -God-wearing, the-Word -is-my-Weapon-toting-Christian! We fasted every Friday with a prayer vigil, and prayed 7 days a week, we had a two-year birthday party for her because we wanted to demonstrate that we were walking by faith and not by sight; believing that God could and would bring her back to us. I tell you this story because it was devastating to me, our family and extended family. Every day we cried, because we could not believe we were losing another one of my chocolate pies. We declared, "Oh no! not this time (the devil is a lie), I would say. We spoke the Word, wrote declarations of the Word and God gave us Grace. We got her back home safely. What an Awesome God!

Faith

One evening early when I was 6 months into my recovery, my kids and I went on a picnic to the Water Wall near Williams Tower in the Houston Galleria area. There was a park across the street with ducks, benches for sitting and an area where we could play and eat. We played and laughed – it was the most fun I had since I was a child. I could laugh, I could feel, I could love again! It was dusk and time for us to leave. I felt the pocket of my pants and it was empty. I had lost my car keys! I said out loud, "Oh no!" I started to panic and was fearful; my son said, "what's wrong?" "I said I have lost the keys to the car, around here somewhere, help me look for them!" We all started looking for the keys everywhere since we had hopped and skipped and ran in the park. The keys could be anywhere! I could not call anyone because there were no telephones anywhere near and cell phones were a luxury back then. I grew more fearful as the lights in the park turned on. I had what the "program" called "a moment of clarity" I remembered one of the members shared in a meeting to say the Serenity Prayer and a 3-word prayer "God help me!" (today I still use that prayer; my husband does the 4-word prayer "God help me now!") I had tears in my eyes, I felt helpless but now hopeless. I was thinking, (stinking thinking) "I just had a good time with my kids and now I have them out here stuck" I said both prayers and in an instance my son yelled, "here they are I found them!" I was relieved and I thanked God! That was my first test of faith and my first miracle in recovery!

Myself

My journey continues, and as I look into the mirror of my own soul, I see a person who is ever-evolving, ever-learning, and ever-growing. I am not defined by my past, but rather by the strength and courage it took to overcome it. And as I move forward, I carry with me the wisdom of my experiences and the promise of a brighter tomorrow.

My Vision

When it comes to my life vision, I asked myself three important questions. First, I wondered, "What do I truly want?" The answer was clear: I want to be the best version of myself and show it to the world.

Next, "What feels right to me?" I imagine writing a book, getting it published, and creating a support system called an Alternative Peer Group and a Recovery High School for young people and families struggling with addiction in a less fortunate area. I envision a support system thriving with the help of funds from famous and local celebrities, business leaders, and Fortune 500 companies. It would be a place where parents would be involved, and resources would be inexhaustible and sustainable.

Then, I thought about what I see myself doing in the future. I envision speaking to people in my community, hosting a podcast, and leading groups for women dealing with substance use, domestic violence, and abuse.

Lastly, I hold a strong belief in my heart: "God is everything or He is nothing," reminding me that faith and divine support are essential on my journey. This belief fuels my determination to grow and help others. Overall, God does for me what I can't do myself.

Flowers of Reflection:

What Do you want? What could feel right for you if you got what you want? What do you see yourself doing in 5,10, 15 years from now? What are some of your beliefs you believe are barriers to your success? What are your beliefs about God or a Higher Power?

Petal Playbook – Time For Action

"Our belief systems are always evident of our experiences" -Louise Hay

1. Take time for self-reflection.
2. Set short- and long-term goals.
3. Explore your interests – try new things and different hobbies.
4. Look for inspiration.
5. Ask yourself questions and answer them honestly.

Words of Encouragement: **In the multitude of my anxieties within me, Your comfort delights my soul (Psalm 94:19 NKJV).**

CHAPTER 5

Overcoming Obstacles and Sowing Seeds of Change

Witness Arnell's triumphs amidst adversity, echoing the resilience of flowers that flourish even in challenging conditions. Just as flowers overcome barriers to bloom, Arnell's determination paves the way for lasting impact.

My Recovery - Adult

The emotions that once defined me were anger, fear, and pain, like old, well-worn companions. Yet, as I've journeyed through recovery, I've unearthed a treasure trove of new feelings and experiences. These newfound emotions have become my guiding stars, helping me navigate the intricate tapestry of life's highs and lows with a newfound sense of purpose and resilience.

Sobriety, a precious gift that mended the painful "hole in my soul" born from the clutches of alcoholism and addiction, has ushered joy into my life. It's a joy that transcends the mere absence of pain; it's a divine gift from God, continuously awakening my spirit. Through the journey of recovery—where I strive to recover, uncover, discover, and discard—I have found success. Yet, success required a fundamental shift in my thinking and belief system. It meant embracing a loving

God, even when I couldn't see or imagine it—a daunting leap into the unknown.

In those moments of uncertainty, my Sponsor's wisdom echoed, urging me to "believe that she believes." This mantra sustained me until my faith in the God of my understanding blossomed. Sometimes, I had to "act as if," as our program suggests, until faith took root.

Seeds of Meditation: What steps can you take to create a fulfilling life transformation?

God has bestowed upon me countless opportunities, and all I must do is remain open to growth, surpassing even my wildest dreams. My journey now leads me to embrace the present, one day at a time, while relinquishing the grip of the past. Whenever fear, anxiety, or resentment knock on the door of my consciousness, I recognize that I may be dwelling in the past or future rather than living in the present moment. I've come to understand that resentments belong to the past, fear is rooted in the future, and anger is an expression of the present. These emotions can manifest as either positive or negative forces, and it's my choice in how I respond to their presence. I am forever grateful for my recovery because it allowed my children to make more informed decisions about having a family, raising children, maintaining their mental health, education, social and spiritual lives. They are awesome young adults living their best lives and being of service to God and others.

Memories: Things I don't Remember; the truth as they saw it, felt it, and heard it

Truth is, there were events in my children's lives I don't remember because of the drug use, anger, and selfishness. Children are indelible and they remember everything you do that makes them feel good or bad about themselves. And it will affect how they see themselves and how they manage their lives. As the good book (Bible) says; "the truth will make you free" Jn 8:32 NKJV so here are a couple of stories from my children:

I remember my first year in 6th grade we were late enrolling. It was early on the first day of school, we were riding around to a few different middle schools in the area near my grandfather's house where we were living. I remember this school that we went to, a Middle School in the community. There was a young lady sitting outside the school in the very front on the steps, and she told my mom ma'am you may not want to bring your son to this school because all they do is fight, cuss, skip school, and this is just not a good school. My mom and I looked at her, continued through the front door, we immediately seen chaos at the front desk. She grabbed my hand, turned me back around, we went back to the car and immediately went to another school where I was able to start with no problems. Where I met the school counselor, who told me that I was welcomed. That day, my mom showed me no matter what, my education matters. I love you very much and I am so blessed and happy that you are my mom.

So, I remember one evening I must have done something I wasn't supposed to, because I was crying and you were upset that I wouldn't stop, so you said "if you don't stop crying, you will be left here while we go get something to eat" my siblings and I had been waiting for you to get home so that we could eat; Daddy (grandfather) was asleep and it was late. I didn't stop crying, so you all got in the car and left me standing in the doorway crying. Daddy never woke up, eventually I stopped crying. I thought you were going to make the block and come back. I think I was already and overthinker because I went through a billion scenarios in my head that never came true. I waited and waited and after nodding off for a brief second, I rationalized that surely you all would bring me something back to eat. I managed to make myself feel better with my logic. After some time, I heard the car pull up. I went to the window I saw you all get out the car come in the door only to find no food for me. The only thing that happened after that was getting put to bed. At that point and my young age, I decided that expect nothing from anyone, my mom did not meet my basic needs which means there is no way you could expect a stranger to meet my needs.

I have so many fond memories with my mom… but I will just give you a few. During my early elementary years, my mom would come into my room every morning before school and would lay her hand on me and pray for me every morning before school, she would also use her fingers as a little bumble bee and make the buzzing sound in my ear to make me smile. I have now started to do that with my son every morning as well. The second memory would most definitely have to be the snow flocked tree that graced our first home together every Christmas. The white flocked tree and blue ornaments were the best! And the last memory I would like to share is the moment my mom decided to quit smoking. I remember it like it was yesterday, I was probably elementary age during this time, as well. We pulled up to the gas station l, and she walked into the gas station to pay for gas and to get her cigarettes, and when she got back into the car, I asked her did she forget to buy her cigarettes and her answer was "no, I quit!" I was so proud of her at that moment.

***Seeds of Meditation:* What types of seeds can initiate positive life changes in your life?**

My dream

I desire to be a beacon of support for children who face unequal opportunities in life. The guiding scripture, "Love your neighbor as yourself," resonates deeply within me, inspiring my mission. I aim for my actions to become an intrinsic part of my identity.

As someone in long-term recovery, 23 years strong, I no longer harbor any desire to turn to illegal substances in any form today. This transformation has fueled my passion for making a difference in the lives of adolescents and their families in my community. I'm moved by the need for accessible and tailored support for those struggling with substance abuse, especially for those who cannot afford in-patient treatment or may not require traditional residential care. My dream is to bridge this gap and offer hope, healing, and a brighter future to those in need.

Living your dream can be challenging because you must seek people who will support your dream, but it can be done.

My Father God is Love and Kind

I would like to share a story that reminds me of God's love for me, along with the following biblical passages:

God is love; and he who abides in love abides in God. 1 John 4:16 NKJV

What is man that You are mindful of him, and the son/daughter of man that you visit him/her? (emphasis added) Psalm 8:4-9 NKJV.

This day reminds me that God loves me and that he comes to my aid and will even visit me. It was another miracle in my life.

He talked to me before, at a time when I began to see him as my father figure. It happened about three years into my recovery program. Back then, I was still trying to grasp the idea of God as my Father, even though I had heard about it in church. It wasn't clear to me.

In Alcoholics Anonymous, they introduced Step 3 as "God as I understand Him/Her," which felt easier to connect with. I was on a journey to learn how to build a relationship with this God I was beginning to understand better. I was driving home from work, and I remember my Sponsor told me, "Just keep praying and asking God to help you understand a relationship". I was meditating on God, and I heard a voice (I had heard this same still small voice when I was two years into recovery) say to me "You don't know me because you think I am like your earthly father." I said, "yes you are right, and I don't trust him because he has let me down so much." I started to tear up and tears were coming down so quickly, I had to pull over then I heard the still small voice say, "I am not like him, I love you and you can trust me." It felt like a huge burden was lifted and I began to believe that God loved me, and I felt loved, and I saw that I was loved. Miracles started happening in my life and a lot of extraordinary things, the supernatural things that only a Spiritual being could understand.

I have learned how to pray, meditate, and talk to God on a regular basis. One morning in Spring of 2016, Good Friday again! I came home from the gym. There were 3 beautiful mallard ducks in my front yard with the prettiest green heads that looked like emeralds. This is significant because I do not live by a pond nor a lake. They were beautiful and I thought about the part of the scripture in Psalms 8:4-9 NKJV, "That You would visit me" I was shocked and in awe of God that they were there in my yard on Good Friday! I was afraid to scare them off, so I did not pull into my driveway. I looked at them a little longer, called my husband and told him "don't open the garage, but look out he front window!" and He did. So, I drove slowly into the driveway and then into the garage. The mallards did not move. I went into the house and looked out the window at them. All I could think of was the Holy Trinity!

***Seeds of Meditation:* What miracles have you encountered as a result of your new beliefs?**

As I stared at them, their backs were to me, one of them began to stand up then the other two stood as well looking up as if they were seeing something! And lo and behold, another mallard flew down from the sky but this one was different. It was brown with no green head. I was crying and praising God! I found out later that brown one was a "female!" Once she landed, long enough for me to see them, they looked at each other and then all four of them took flight! By this time, tears filled my eyes. God has shown me many times that my little girl, Cricket, is okay and is doing His Will! It was as if Cricket said "Mom I'm with them and I am Okay! God loved me enough that He shared Good Friday with me, his grief, and his sorrow.

3 ducks mallards in my front yard.

4 ducks mallards joined by the brown one in my front yard.

Flowers of Reflection:

In what ways do your beliefs exert a constraining or lingering influence on your life?

Could you share the habits you've cultivated when faced with beliefs from your past and present that appear to hinder your future?

Petal Playbook – Time For Action

In order to create a more fulfilling and empowered life, we have to be equipped to address and transform limiting beliefs and habits.

1. Challenge and questions your beliefs
2. Replace limiting beliefs with empowering ones
3. Cultivate positive habits
4. Seek support and accountability

Words of encouragement: **And we know that all things work together for good to those who love God, to those who are the called according to *His* purpose (Romans 8:28 NKJV).**

CHAPTER 6

Embracing New Beginnings: Retirement and Legacy

Experience Arnell's transition into retirement, marking the close of one chapter and the dawn of another. Reflection becomes a guiding light as she contemplates her life's journey. Here, the art of giving flowers takes on a new dimension, symbolizing the wisdom and experiences she shares with others.

First Professional Job

In 1983 a task force was formed to investigate how to bring 9-1-1 to community and surrounding counties. In the Communications department, where I was employed, were members of the task force. As the communications installations clerk for our county government Communications department, I was asked attended each meeting to ensure that the recording equipment was working properly and to record each meeting as presentations were given from other 9-1-1 agencies and local (police, fire and EMS), vendors, telephone companies and wireless providers from around the country and state.

In November 1983, the citizens voted unanimously for the 9-1-1 Referendum. In April 1984, the administrative office for 9-1-1 was established. There were six employees: the Executive Director,

Operations Manager, Database Manager, Office Manager, and my position as secretary and later, Database Assistant.

My biggest challenge: When I was promoted to Database and Administrative Staff Manager, which entailed greater responsibilities working with and managing a team of five employees. I also became more involved working with an GIS and IT department, which today is considered one of the first Phase II wireless 9-1-1 agencies in the country and the first to implement wireless in Texas.

My Next Challenge Was

In 2004, I moved forward with sharing a vision with the Deputy Director that would vastly change internal and external geographical foot- print in the state. After receiving the necessary buy-in and technical support from all of the stakeholders, and following countless research and implementation hours, this vision became a reality on November 17, 2008

My greatest success: Attending and completing Rice University, Jones School of Business Management and earning my Emergency Number Professional certification working with Vendors, AT&T team of administrators, the Database/GIS Managers and State 911 President. It is exciting to be a part of something bigger than you and to see it to a successful conclusion.

My challenges: Personally, it was running for office on the State's National Emergency Number (911) Association for board Secretary, VP and President and won. I took on the challenge and succeeded in leading one of the largest state chapters in the organization. It has provided me new experiences and I have learned more about myself as a person and others.

My former position was to keep up with the new technology that is being introduced on a daily basis, as well as keeping people working together with the goal of improving services and saving lives.

Leisure time: Taking time for prayer and reading a good mind-stimulating book with a cup of hot tea. Participating in family discussions with my handsome and supportive husband and loving children.

Retirement

I saw that job as a career (and it was a dream come true) that I would grow and move up in the industry. However, it came to a halt when the department director decided to do a re-organization of staff duties and responsibilities. I believed it was a good time to retire after 28 years; I was then catapulted to the best success in my life! To actually live another dream! I learned after many years of deception and disappointments how I stay in harmful situations and relationships too long. God showed me and I since learned how to reset and recreate myself. I now have enough wisdom and insight to see when a relationship whether it's personal or professional is harmful or not fulfilling and I can end them rather than being forced out of a situation or another person ending the relationship. (I saw the writing on the wall, flags and signs but ignored them).

January 28, 2011 retiring at age 53 from a Director's position and career in telecommunications, to a new beginning in my life. I see this as someone put it "retiring to something, rather than retiring from something." I always had a desire to write a book that would make a difference in someone's life. I have always had a commitment to improving my world through community service. It was suggested that I write a book about retirement; and my experience, the dos and the don'ts but I am certainly not the expert on that topic. However, I can share my experience, strength and hope in that area. I said "It will be interesting when my husband retires May 31, 2011 as well; we will both have some experiences and some lessons on do's and don'ts to share."

"Nothing, absolutely nothing happens
in God's world by mistake."
-Alcoholic Anonymous

"You either walk inside your story and
own it or you stand outside your story
and hustle for your worthiness."
-Brené Brown

Memorials: God's Gifts and Blessings

April and October are important months in my life because they hold special memories of my daughter, Lakeisha Renee, whom I lovingly called "Cricket," and the blessings that God has given me.

Month of April – Easter, my birth month (20th), Good Friday - Cricket's heavenly homegoing
April 2 - My second daughter's birthdate
April 16 - God's blessings of assurance (the Ducks came to visit)!
April 19 – My first-born son walked the day of my daughter's viewing, and it is the day before my 19th birthday.
April 27 – Birthdate of my bonus daughter
Month of October – Cricket's birthdate (October 11), her father's birthdate (October 18)
October 10 – Birthdate of my bonus son
Significance of 33 – Age 33 – Jesus' ministry and age 30 and died age 33 (mu understanding) - my old life died and I was reborn at age 33, 2023 – 33 years of abstinence and living a life of peace

I was reading a meditation from the book "Stepping Stones" dated August 31, 2023, called "Today's Gift". It talked about how when we put words to what has happened to us, we can begin to learn from our experiences. We carry images that are the building blocks of our stories, but we only begin to make sense of them when we put them into words…the words give us a way to understand, and they build a bridge to others.

***Seeds of Meditation:* What areas of your life do you seek transformation or change?**

We may feel deeply alone if we keep our memories and images to ourselves. When we begin to talk, as we tell our story, we learn from our own words, and they take us deeper into our truth. We don't tell our story only once. We do it repeatedly. It brings relief from traumas and releases us from the prison of our past. Today as I have grown, I can see my story from a new perspective.

Flowers of Reflection:

As you reflect on your life, what days or months hold special significance in your life?

What aspects of your personal story do you believe can lead you to a deeper understanding of your truth and provide relief from past traumas?

Petal Playbook – Time For Action

In the journey of self-discovery and healing, our stories serve as powerful guides. These actions empower us to explore our narratives, seek support and reframe our perspectives about ourselves and our relationships.

1. Identify key stories and narratives from your past
2. Explore your thoughts, feelings and experiences at the time.
3. Seek guidance and support
4. Reinterpret and reframe your narratives
5. As you integrate these new perspectives, use them as tools for healing and personal transformation.

Words of Comfort: **Your eyes saw my substance, being yet unformed. And in your book, they all were written. The days fashioned for me. When as yet there were none of them. (Psalm 139:16 NKJV)**

CHAPTER 7

Empowerment in Full Bloom: Impacting Lives

Delve into Arnell's initiatives, including the Alternative Peer Group and Recovery High School. Collaboration with communities and luminaries amplifies her message of empowerment. The art of giving flowers blooms as a representation of her transformative effect on inner-city adolescents, women, and families as they too flourish against the odds.

Impacting lives in a positive way is like planting a garden and watching the flowers and plants grow into beautiful flowers and knowing you are part of that growth is fulfilling. As I offer my prayers, experience, strength, and growth into each person's life, I get the benefit of watching their growth and success. The program teaches us that "we can't keep what we have unless we give it away." In other words, "pay it forward." I am also reminded of the scripture, "Every branch in Me that does not bear fruit He takes away.; and every branch that bears fruit He prunes, that I may bear more fruit. John 15:2 NKJV. Every person loves to receive gifts, or affirmations, accolades for themselves as much as possible. But when you give a part of yourself without expecting to receive something in return, you receive a joy that is unimaginable, unspeakable, and full of God's glory! And you get more in return.

***Seeds of Meditation:* What do you desire to do in your life to impact others with your gifts and talents?**

As Dr. Charles Stanley puts it when he talks about the law of reaping and sowing; "you reap what you sow, more than you sow and longer than you sow!" (Emphasis added) We really do live in an abundant universe, and our giving results in experiencing God's abundance. (The lack is between our ears – what we speak to ourselves). I used to think that everyone thought like I did, or they should think like I do. (smile). I also thought they had the same feelings about life. I had to realize and accept that I am different from other people, this has been a knowing all my life and it's ok. We are not all the same. I remind myself often of the many good qualities I have and the blessings of family, friends, and colleagues.

A Time to Change

I originally was going to name this book, "A Time to Change" in an appreciation for the inspiration and direction from God the Father, my Lord and Savior Jesus Christ and His amazing Holy Spirit and it is the name of our Charity.

Hundreds of thousands of people are sick and dying from the "evil corroding disease" called Alcoholism and Addiction which I believe is one of and has been the biggest pandemics for a long time. Another pandemic that has changed our perspective is the Corona Virus – 19 or COVID.

Today, COVID has changed our entire lives, how we live and move about the world. My belief is that millions will live and recover from this disease as well as the disease of alcoholism and drug addiction. My hope is that everyone will be inspired by a *Power greater than themselves.* And that power which I call God is exemplified in their daily living, *One day at a time and one moment at a time.*

"Dwelling on our pain is unproductive...however we do need to identify the pain, give it attention, and then be willing to let it go. Naming it sheds light on it preventing the pain from living in the shadows where

it remains free to haunt us. Life is never wholly free from struggle and pain. As a part of the human community, we learn significant lessons... But letting our steps be guided (ordered by God; ref. the Bible) by a power greater than ourselves. i.e., Higher Power instead of fearfully resisting that Power, will make our lessons easier to learn and our journey smoother. (Inspiration from "A Woman's Spirit")

We have learned, grown, changed...we did what we needed to do then. If we made mistakes, we cannot let it stop us from living and fully experiencing our lives today. We have arrived at the understanding that we needed our experiences, even our mistakes to get to where we are today.

Do we know that we needed or life to unfold exactly as it did to find ourselves, God, and this new way of life? Or is part of us still calling our past a mistake? (Language of Letting Go. M. Beatty, pg.299, October 18)

Flowers of Reflection:

How has your life changed since the latest pandemic? What changes have you made to be successful?

Petal Playbook – Time for Action:

Think about what changes you need to make in your life by asking the following questions:

1. What aspects of my life am I currently unhappy with?
2. What are my long-term goals and aspirations?
3. What habits or behaviors are barriers to my growth and success?

***Words of Comfort:* ...For when I am weak, then I am strong (2 Corinthians 12:10 NKJV).**

THE FLOWER GARDEN

These pages echo Arnell's journey from desolation to empowerment. The art of giving flowers stands as a testament to the beauty that arises from compassion and connection. You are invited to embrace the power of transformation, weaving the art of giving flowers into your own life and creating your own flower Garden of love and appreciation.

May Arnell's journey's lessons inspire an awakening of your own inner garden, blooming with resilience, empowerment, and the enduring beauty of giving.

Affirmations

af·firm·a·tion – Noun.

1. something that is affirmed; a statement or proposition that is declared to be true. confirmation or ratification of the truth or validity of a prior judgment, decision, etc.
2. emotional support or encouragement.
   "the lack of one or both parents' affirmation leaves some children emotionally crippled."

An affirmation is anything you say or think. -Louise Hay
Affirmations are positive statements designed for repeated listening,

a sort of reprogramming of your unconscious mind to combat negative thinking. -Bellruth Naparstek

Biblical Affirmations

Affirmations are an important part of my prayer life.

Prayers of affirmation is a way of telling *ourselves* things that are true and helpful knowing that God listens. Affirmations are also a way of obeying the command to focus on the scripture "finally....whatever is true, whatever is noble, whatever is right, whatever is pure, whatever is lovely, whatever is admirable, if there is any if anything is excellent or praiseworthy – think about such things" (Philippians 4:8 NIV).

1. The Lord is my shepherd; I lack nothing (Psalm 23:1 NIV).
2. The Lord is my light and my salvation— whom shall, I fear? The LORD is the stronghold of my life— of whom shall I be afraid? (Psalm 27:1 NIV).
3. When my anxious thoughts multiply within me. Your comfort delights my soul (Psalm 94:19 NKJV).
4. My help comes from the Lord, the Maker of heaven and earth (Psalm 121:2 NIV).
5. In all things God works for the good of those who love him, who have been called according to his purpose (Romans 8:28 NIV).
6. When I am weak, then I am strong (2 Corinthians 12:10 NIV).
7. Be strong in the Lord and in his mighty power (Ephesians 6:10 NIV).
8. The eyes of the Lord are on the righteous and his ears are attentive to their prayer (1 Peter 3:12 NIV).

Flowers of Reflection:

How do you want to be remembered?
What is your Life's Journey and Purpose?
Are you willing to ask your tribe to contribute to your legacy?

Petal Playbook – Time for Action

1. Remember that how you want to be remembered is closely tied to your actions.
2. Consider ways to leave a lasting impact, whether through your work, relationships, or contributions to your community

Words of Comfort: We will not hide them from their descendants; we will tell the next generation the praiseworthy deeds of the Lord, his power, and the wonders he has done (Psalm 78:4 NIV)

MY AFFIRMATIONS

I have everything I need, and it comes from places I never imagined.
I love my mother as she is (even if she does
not show up as I would like her to)
I live with the solution, rather than the problem.
God is my source and resource.
I am not hurting myself today with substances.
It's ok to learn.
I am healed from the disease of addiction.
I have a principled-centered life.
I live by principles of honesty, purity, patience, self-control.

Powerful Affirmations

I am safe.
I am always taken care of
I have everything that I need right here at this moment.
There is only one of me.
My clients need what I have to offer.
I have gifts and talents that are important to this world.
–Jen Sincero

I will know love when I realize loving myself helps to resolve the things that make me feel bad.
I am willing to acknowledge a little girl needs a father to help her grow into a woman.
I am now receptive to the idea that the need to be liked reflects what needs to be healed.
"I am now willing to forgive myself for not taking time to deal with certain unpleasant memories." –yanla Vanzant

There are no limits to your ability to think. You can imagine yourself doing anything.
You are not a human being having a spiritual experience; You are a spiritual being having a human experience. –Pierre Teilhard de Chardin

"You'll See It When You Believe It." -Wayne Dyer
"When you change the way, you look at things, the things you look at changes." –Wayne Dyer

Five Guiding Principles to Live by Dr. Charles Stanley

1. The most important thing in your life is your relationship with God.
2. Obey God and leave al the consequences to Him.
3. God will move heaven and earth to reveal His will to you if you really want to know it and do it.
4. God will provide for all your needs.
5. God will protect you.

Give Me Flowers so I Can Live

My Flower Garden

I liken flowers to words of love and affirmation that are given to me - these words are heartfelt gifts to me. As a part of my own evolution of healing, I have created a sacred space in my life, full of loving words, scriptures, and affirmations from those who love, support and care for me. I called this space, My Flower Garden. I invite you to read the following words of love, appreciation, affirmation and inspired scriptures – flowers I received as I live:

Scripture: 1Thessalonians 5:11 NIV Therefore encourage one another and build each other up, just as in fact you are doing.

Flowers: "Arnell Evans, you are forever encouraging, and a resilient pursuer of life-changing opportunities. Not just for your family, but for any and everyone who wants better for themselves and their family. Thank you for loving me the way God intended!"

Scripture: Psalm 55:22 NIV Give your burdens to the Lord, and he will sustain you.

Flowers: "It will always work out, why, because it always does!" I must admit I hated it when you would say this, I wanted you to tell me what I should do during my time of struggle. I wanted you to fix it for me! You were teaching me to lean on God. Thank you, you have and always will be the perfect mother for me! I Love You!"

Matthew 11:30 NIV For my yoke is easy and my burden is light.

Affirmation: Lay all your burdens on God because he can handle them all. Let Him be the shoulder where you can rest!

Affirmation: One of the truest forms of love is to be and feel seen. Effortlessly you have always provided a safe space for me to come to you and receive that. No matter the time or space of my journey, home is and has always been home with you. There's a different level of peace that you provide for the people you love, and it's always felt like this blanket of protection. I love you. I'm grateful for you. I'm proud of you.

Flowers: When you came into our family, I was too young to know anything. But as time went on, I realized how lucky I am to have you in my life. Your positive influence shines through in the little things you do for so many people. Your comforting presence during the important moments in my life, your encouraging words in times of doubt, and your unconditional love has provided me with a foundation that has helped me to grow in this world. Your support in my dreams and ambitions has been invaluable. Your belief in me has given me the courage to chase my goals and knowing that you have my back pushes me to reach for the stars. You have seamlessly blended our families' unique personalities and differences, creating a loving environment for all of us to thrive in.

Flowers: Thank you for being an incredible role model and for loving me unconditionally. You have shown me what it means to be selfless, compassionate, and kind. I am truly blessed to have you in my life, and I look forward to creating many more cherished memories together.

With all my love and appreciation,

Scripture: Matthew 5:25 NIV "Settle matters quickly with your adversary who is taking you to court."

Flowers: A reliable source for me to reflect internally employing the reconcilable attitude under duress or distress.

Scripture: Deuteronomy 4:9 NIV Only be careful and watch yourselves closely so that you do not forget the things your eyes have seen or let them fade from your heart as long as you live. Teach them to your children and to their children after them.

Flowers: My Grandmother is one of the most goal-driven, caring and thoughtful people I know. The way she takes on situations and finds resources for individuals including her own family members is incredible. I've always thought her way of empathizing with someone to be influential because she is a great listener with impartial advice. She's a kind person who loves her family and her willingness to help others is shown through her career and her community outreach youth programs. I'm thankful for my grandmother and what she has taught me and shown me in this lifetime, for that I will always be grateful. It's a quote that I read by Leo Buscaglia, "Too often we underestimate the power of a touch, a smile, a kind word, a listening ear, an honest compliment, or the smallest act of caring, all of which have the potential to turn a life around."

Flowers: My grandmother has always instilled in me the importance of prayer. Thanks to her I am stronger in my faith. She also makes sure I know my worth and never allows me, nor anyone I've witnessed her interact with, to feel less than. I love you

Flowers: If someone asked me to describe you in two words, I'd say "Beautiful & Amazing"

You are Beautiful, Psalm 139:14, Chosen 1 Peter 2:9, Made For A Purpose Ephesians 2:10

A Presious Child Of God, John 1:12, Loved Forever, Jeremiah 31:3

Scripture: Proverbs 3:13-18NIV

Blessed is those who find wisdom, those who gain understanding, for she is more profitable than silver and yields better returns than gold. She is more precious than rubies; nothing you desire can compare with her. Long life is in her right hand; in her left hand are riches and honor. Her ways are pleasant ways, and all her paths are peace. She is a tree of life to those who take hold of her; those who hold her fast will be blessed.

Affirmation: Your heart, aura, and energies are unmatched. It feels so positive whenever you are around.

Affirmation: Arnell you are beautiful, kind, caring spirit. I am thankful to have made your acquaintance!

Scripture: Matthew 6:28-32NIV

Affirmation: "You may have to fight a battle more than once to win." Margaret Thatcher

"Do no harm but take no bull."

Scripture: Colossians 3:12 NIV "Therefore, as God's chosen people, holy and dearly loved, clothe yourselves with compassion, kindness, humility, gentleness and patience."

Affirmation: I affirm that you are compassionate towards others. Thank you for showing compassion towards my family.

Scripture: Psalms 59:16 NIV "But I will sing of your strength, in the morning, I will sing of your love; for you are my fortress, my refuge in times of trouble."

Affirmation: You trust yourself. Your inner wisdom guides you.

Affirmation: You are my champion! You won't give up on me, we have a connection, and you push me to be the best I can be! "Every child deserves a champion; an adult wo will never give up on them, who understands the power of connection and insists that they become the best they can possibly be." Rita F. Pierson

"Show me a successful individual and I'll show you someone who had real positive influences in his or her life. I don't care what you do for a living—if you do it well, I'm sure there was someone cheering you on or showing the way. A mentor." — *Denzel Washington*

Scripture: John 8:36 NIV So, if the Son sets you free, you will be free indeed

Affirmation: I am worthy! I can hear you saying it and embracing it!

Scripture: Psalm 23 NIV

Flowers: The way I see Arnell Evans has always been the same. Although she has always reached higher heights for herself to help those in need especially her babies and definitely for me that means me as an adult as well. I am forever grateful for her taking me under her wings and loving me unconditionally. I have to express Arnell Evans in this manner.

A Always available for myself as well as others for the need is never too small or big.
R Respectful to herself and others always.
N No is never an option for me/family when I need her most. No matter day or night.
E Endurance is an understatement for her ability to stay the course.
L Loving with a listening ear.

L Loyal and dedicated to her mission and those she love.

Flowers: You are ALWAYS there with encouragement, to listen, and to share. God placed you in my Life for a reason- HE knew you cared... I needed that even before I knew it. During the season of us physically being together daily, I lost my oldest brother Anthony and my Big Sis - Carol. God knew I would need "replacement family "and I'm thankful He gave You!

"Try the spirit, by the Spirit" that's what you are to me. Wisdom and an "on time" Word. I thank God for you and I Thank You for being you! Being Real — priceless.

Scripture: Ephesians 2:10 NIV We are God's Masterpiece

Flowers: You always see the best in others. It's really refreshing to be around you. Your positivity is contagious.

Flowers: I just want you to know that you have been an inspiration in my life. I've never met anyone do caring and knowledgeable about helping people. You have become a great friend of mine, and I will cherish it always.

Flowers: The epitome of class, elegance, grace & poise, and the living example of genuineness, kindness, patience, and selflessness - thank you for being these things and so much more! The Bible gives us clear expectations around who we are called to be as friends in Proverbs 27:17. Thank you for being an iron sharpener to so many, including myself. Thank you for allowing others to learn from you at times where you yourself may need it most. Your wisdom, consideration, and overall pure acts of kindness does not go unnoticed. In the words of the Golden Girls, "Thank you for being a friend!" Keep walking in the light and radiating amongst others!

Scripture:

Matthew 18:19 NIV Again, truly I will tell you that if two of you on earth agree about anything they ask for, it will be done for them by my Father in heaven.

Hebrews 13:2 NIV Do not forget to show hospitality to strangers, for by so doing some people have shown hospitality to angels without knowing it.

Flowers: It only takes one person, and one act of kindness, to inspire others and create change.

You are the epitome of this. You help in your giving, caring, loving, encouragement, and honesty; you will also share your experience, strength, and hope; in addition to your time for various people, places, and situations. Then to put the cherry on top, you will pray with and for all. Thank you for always being a part of and not apart from. That makes you a very powerful woman of God and a force to be with. "Remember there's no such thing as a small act of kindness. Every act creates a ripple with no logical end" – Scott Adams

Scripture: Joshua 1:9 NIV Be strong and courageous. Do not be afraid; do not be discouraged, for the Lord your God will be with you wherever you go.

Flowers: You bring joy and positivity to my life, and your friendship is a true blessing. Believe you can, and you're halfway there." - Theodore Roosevelt

Scripture: Psalm 139:14 NIV, I will praise thee; for I am fearfully and wonderfully made: marvelous are thy works; and that my soul know full well.

Flowers: You are kind, considerate, giving of yourself and present.

Flowers: You are one of my most favorite people on this earth. And do you know why? It's because you are genuine. The real deal. You are smart, kind, loving and compassionate. I most admire that as you grow you teach. I love you because you are trustworthy, confident and a safe space. You always share your wisdom, experience, strength, and hope. You are brutally honest sometimes. Not everybody knows how to appreciate your honesty in the moment. If they knew like I know they would realize that all that honesty comes from an expansive love and desire for others to find their way. Mostly because you are a living example of what happens when you let the truth set you free.

Scripture: Matthew 5:16 NIV ...Let your light so shine before others, that they may see your good works, and glorify your Father which is in heaven.

Flowers: Your spirit is a bright light that shines for the world to see and experience. Your faith, and faithfulness, are on front street for all to see. I am one of your #1 fans because you are my sister for life.

Scripture: Romans 15:4 NIV For everything that was written in the past was written to teach us, so that through the endurance taught in the Scriptures and the encouragement; Matthew 22:37 NIV, "Jesus replied, Love the Lord your God with all your heart and with all your soul and with all your mind."

Flowers: Hope in the Lord! You have taught me to come honestly and unabashedly to the Lord. I've watched you place your whole heart into Him when you were hurting, disappointed or confused. You always come to Him just as you are. I see you as His daughter who loves the Lord with everything you have. It's who you are. Nothing to hide. Pure love. Thank you for being such a beautiful example for me of what that looks like as I have watched you throughout my own journey with the Lord.

Scripture: 1 Thessalonians 5:11 NIV "Therefore encourage one another and build one another up, just as in fact you are doing."

Flowers: You with grace, unapologetically, share your journey to encourage others. When I say to you, "I want to be like you when I grow up", you say, "Don't be like me, be better!"

Affirmations: I am equally as worthy as everyone else, My worth is not determined by the outcome., I give my time and energy mindfully, I am joyfully embracing each new day with gratitude.

Scripture: Jeremiah 29:11NLT For I know the plans I have for you," declares the Lord. "Plans to prosper you and not to harm you, plans to give you hope and a future."

Affirmation: Mrs Arnell's is an extension of God. Her dedication to her sobriety, her family, friends, and those she serves is admirable and greatly appreciated. Mrs Arnell has the gift of service and ministry.

Her unwavering commitment to each of the aforementioned is a gift back to us and it is appreciated and demonstrated on a daily basis. Mrs Arnell has used her experience, strength, and hope to uplift, encourage, minister, and heal. Her lack of fear to tell you the truth makes me trust her. Her smile and her tone helps you to receive whatever you're seeking whether it's counseling or advice. To have her as a part of my life is a treasure.

Mrs Arnell has helped me in my recovery, and I am eternally grateful. If an opportunity arises for her to befriend you or receive counseling from her - take it. It will be life changing. Mrs Arnell is one of the kindest, most hospitable, honest, loyal, wise, dependable, committed, and dedicated people I have had the pleasure of knowing. Our relationship has brought healing and encouragement to my life. May God continue to give her strength and encouragement to continue to carry out his plan so she can be blessed and be a blessing to others.

Flowers: I see you as a person that can walk the walk as she talks it. You do not have to wonder where you are coming from, because you are transparent by God's own design. God Blessed me by putting you in my life at the right day and hour! Glory be to God! God knew I'd needed a true friend at that time, so He sent me you.

Scripture: Isaiah 26:4 NIV- Trust in the Lord forever because in the Lord the Lord himself is the Rock eternal.

Flowers: I see you as a confidant, a person who gives an honest opinion. A person who's not afraid to try, to receive constructive criticism. A person who loves hard, fights for her family and friends. You are giving, funny, walks with integrity. You are the person that I want in my corner forever and always. Remember you can do ALL things through CHRIST which strengthens you.

Scripture: Ruth 1:16-17 NIV Where you go, I will go; where you stay, I will stay; your people shall be my people, and your God my God.

Flowers: When I think of you Arnell Renee Evans, I think of a beautiful gift. I then thank God for giving me such a beautiful gift. You are more than a friend to me. You a more than a sister, confidante, or mentor. I can hardly put this love into words. It is as hard as trying to describe God's love for us, yet it is as easy as describing God's love for us. You are passionate, dedicated, kind, caring, intuitive, and compassionate. Describing our union is like telling someone about the love that Jesus has for us. We are not Thelma and Louise; we are like Ruth and Naomi.

May God continue to use us as examples of His incredible love, grace, and kindness. We are More Than Friends – we are sisters!

Scripture: Psalm 139:14 NIV, I praise you because I am fearfully and wonderfully made; your works are wonderful; I know that full well.

Flowers: Arnell is a great listener and encourager and willing to do what she can to support her friends.

Affirmation: I do not need to be perfect to be valuable

Scripture: Jeremiah 29:11 NIV For I know the plans I have for you," declares the Lord, "plans to prosper you and not to harm you, plans to give you hope and a future.

Flowers: I see you as wise counsel; a person who has lived and has the scars to prove it, but one who is transparent and willing to share to help the next person and bring glory and honor to God.

Scripture: 1 John 4:20 NIV, Whoever claims to love God, yet hates a brother or sister is a liar; for if we don't love people we can see, how can we love God, whom we cannot see?

Flowers: You preach love and light. This scripture is in the light that emanates from you.

Flowers: Arnell is the kind of person that you do not have to know for a long time to realize that she has a wonderful personality. She is warm and friendly and loves interacting with people. She is loving and caring and kind. She reaches out to others especially if she sees a need. She is professional, yet down to earth and can relate to your situations. Arnell is spiritually anchored and is equipped to handle life's challenges. Indeed, she is a person I am happy to call a friend.

Scripture: Proverbs 17:17 NIV - "A friend loves at all times, and a brother is born for a time of adversity."

Flowers: Your presence in my life has been a constant source of inspiration, joy, and support, and I am immensely grateful for the countless ways you've positively impacted my journey.

One of the things that stand out the most when I think of you is your unwavering and unconditional acceptance. From the very moment we became friends, you embraced me with love and open arms, and that acceptance has been a transformative force in my life. Your ability to show love and acceptance, no matter the circumstances, has helped me bloom and blossom into the woman I am today.

You are a beacon of light and strength, always ready to lift others up and spread kindness wherever you go. Your unwavering love and genuine care have touched not only my life but the lives of so many others around you. Your friendship has been a blessing beyond measure, and I am truly blessed to have you by my side through thick and thin.

Your resilience in facing challenges, your empathy towards others, and your unwavering faith have been a shining example for me. You have taught me the power of hope, the value of friendship, and the beauty of unwavering trust in God's plan.

In times of doubt or difficulty, you have been a steadfast presence, reminding me to keep my head high and my heart strong. Your encouragement has lifted me up when I felt low, and your unwavering belief in me has been a constant motivation to strive for my dreams.

As I think of you, a verse from the Bible comes to mind, and I believe it speaks to the incredible person you are and the deep impact you've had on my life:

You have embodied this verse in every way. Your love, acceptance, loyalty, and support have been a foundation of strength for me, and I am so grateful to have you as not just a friend but also a sister through thick and thin.

Flowers: You have been more than a friend...a true confidant. You helped me survive. I am truly thankful for you.

Scriptures: Proverbs 20:6 NIV Many claim to have unfailing love, but a faithful person who can find? Proverbs 27:9 NIV The heartfelt counsel of a friend is as sweet as perfume and incense.Proverbs 27:17 NIV As iron sharpens iron, so one person sharpens another.

Scripture: Philippians 4:13 NIV, I can do all things through Christ who strengthens me.

Flowers: In the words of the song by Bill Withers "You Just Call My name" and wherever you are I come running to be there again. Arnell is that kind of friend, winter. Spring summer or fall all you have to do is call and she will be there to love on you, support you and pray for you. A friend indeed with a bountiful gift to love family, friends, the community, and the God she serves.

Scripture: Psalms 46:5 NIV God is within her; she shall not fail; God will help her at break of day.

Flowers: Woman of GOD - Loyal, Dedicated to Family, Friends, and her Community

Scripture: Luke 10:30-37 NIV

Flowers: When I think of Arnell the story of the Good Samaritan comes to mind. She has the heart to see the need of a person and the compassion that provides them with love and mercy. Arnell is truly sincere in her quest to help others not in a way where she comes off as a "holier than thou" personality but with kindness and sincerity. This makes her not only a good friend but a faithful wife, loving mother, devoted grandmother and a child and servant of the One True and Living God.

Scripture: 1 Corinthians 15:58 NIV Therefore, my dear brothers and sisters, stand firm. Let nothing move you. Always give yourselves fully to the work of the Lord, because you know that your labor in the Lord is not in vain.

Flowers: Your presence in my life has been such a blessing, and I am grateful for the love and support you constantly show. Your genuine kindness and compassion inspire me to be a better person. I truly value and appreciate the amazing woman you are.

Flowers: I thank the Lord for you, Arnell! I will always remember you as the first person in my life to say, "Who's taking care of you?" I was actually taken aback about the thought. It never occurred to me that I even needed "taking care of." Thank you for taking the time to work with me and to help me realize that being hurt is a feeling that I can feel. Thank you for guiding me and allowing me to share my pain. Thanks for keeping it real! I appreciate you and will always cherish our sisterhood and friendship.

You are beautiful, but not just because of your appearance. You are beautiful because of the light you carry within you." – Alexandra Elle

Scripture: Galatians 5:22 NIV But the fruit of the Spirit is love, joy, peace, forbearance, kindness, goodness, faithfulness, gentleness, and self-control. Against such things there is no law.

Flowers: When I think about you, the first thing that came to mind is what a beautiful gift from God you are to me and countless others. Your smile truly lights up the room and your honesty and strength are inspirations to me. Arnell, I thank God for you. Keep on shining, keep on growing and keep on blooming. You exemplify this Bible verse, one of my favorites.

Flowers: You are one of a kind, a woman who takes care of her own and bless so many on your special journey. Once again, I would like to take the time to thank you for the wisdom and knowledge you have given me over the 7 years. As my Counselor, but everyone knows you're the young Grandma in my life. Your strength and kindness have pushed me to be a role model for the youth just like you have done for so many including me. I'm so proud of you and your work.

Keep up the good work. Always take one day at a time. Don't let the behaviors of others destroy the inner you.

Flowers: You are an amazing leader, loving wife, and caring mother. A highly educated woman who kills people with kindness and I love that about you. There are so many things I am grateful for, and you are one of them because you took me under your wing when I pushed you away so many times but you saw something in me that I didn't see myself. God sent you to me at the right time. I had so much anger built up inside of me but those morning sessions and teaching us the serenity prayer taught me that everything is not in my control, and I have to learn to let things go because everything happens for a reason. Ever since then you have been in my life for the better, so I thank you for that. Thank you for your time, I don't take it for granted and thank you for the love and support when I needed it most. I couldn't have asked for a better mentor/ Godmother.

"God Grant me the serenity to accept the things we cannot change, the courage to change the things we can and the wisdom to know the difference."

Flowers: Arnell brought change and joy in the life of my brother, Bert. She loves and supports him and shows a real and profound appreciation for him which in turn makes him respond to be the man that God called him to be. Our mother felt comfortable leaving him in her loving care. She's my sister in love and has been a Godly presence in this family and a loving role model for their children. May she continue to soar to new heights and continue to make us proud. We love you, N

Flowers: Arnell is beautiful inside and out with the heart of a warrior. Life hasn't been easy, but through her faith in God she knows she can handle anything life has thrown at her. She loves her family and would do anything to keep them safe and happy.

"Strong women don't play victim, don't make themselves look pitiful, and don't point fingers. They stand and they deal." Mandy Hale

Scripture: Have I not commanded you? Be strong and courageous. Do not be afraid; do not be discouraged, for the Lord your God will be with you wherever you go."

Joshua 1:8 NIV *Flowers: Some of the strongest people are not the ones that show their strength in front of you but win battles we know nothing about. Arnell, you have a heart of gold. What you have silently accomplished to help so many is a blessing and a story that should be told. I am so honored to have you as a role model and a sister-in-love.*

Flowers: My auntie Arnell is a loving, generous, and kind person who freely gives and receives universal abundance, living, loving, and giving with joy.

Scripture: Hebrew11:1 NIV, Now Faith is the confidence in what we hope for and assurance about what we do not see.

Flowers: Arnell is a motivational speaker for sure. Arnell can make you feel much better when you are at your lowest. Arnell is definitely a leader. She's been leading for a while now. I feel comfortable and confident with her in the front of my line leading. I trust her. She has always stepped up to take charge. Arnell is awesome.

Flowers: When I think of Arnell, I think of how Awesome and Powerful God can be in your life if you let him in! Arnell reminds me to forgive my younger self and past mistakes and no matter what I may go through just like my Big Sister Arnell Still I rise!

Flowers of Reflection:

How have affirmations impacted your life, if at all? Have you ever used affirmations as a tool for personal growth or positivity?

Petal Playbook – Time for Action

1. Daily Affirmation Practice: If you're open to it, consider incorporating daily affirmations into your routine. Start your day by reciting positive statements that resonate with your goals and aspirations. This simple practice can set a positive tone for your day
2. Journaling Affirmations: Another approach is to keep an affirmation journal. Write down your chosen affirmations and reflect on how they make you feel. Over time, you might notice patterns and shifts in your mindset.

Words of Comfort: **Truly I tell you, if anyone says to this mountain, 'Go, throw yourself into the sea,' and does not doubt in their heart but believes that what they say will happen, it will be done for them. (Mark 11:23 NIV)**

Your Flower Garden

Imagine a garden of beautiful affirmations, scriptures, and kind words, each one representing a unique bond between you and your loved ones. This garden, nurtured with love and care, can bloom into something truly remarkable. It is about fostering connections that are rooted in love and affirmation and it starts with this simple request.

A Call to Action

I encourage you to cultivate your own flower garden and ask 10 people in your life to send you some encouraging words of love. Let love bloom in your life.

Bible… be a doer of the word not just a hearer only
12 Step Program…is a Spiritual program of action
Love… is an action word

In Loving Memory of LaKeisha Renee'
"Cricket"

Disclaimer: While I don't hold the title of a Theologian or profess expertise in the intricate interpretations of Bible scriptures, I do wish to impart my personal journey, resilience, and inspiration derived from my connection to Jesus Christ (my higher power). As a dedicated Bible student with the wealth of experience, including the facilitation of numerous Bible study groups, I humbly share my insights and reflections in this book.

ABOUT THE AUTHOR

Arnell Evans, a Licensed Chemical Dependency Counselor, Speaker, and Entrepreneur, contributed her insights to the documentary "Generation Found." Hailing from the heart of Texas, Arnell's mission is deeply spiritual, transcending religious boundaries. Her perspectives are born from her interpretation of the word of God, her personal relationship with the Divine, and her assimilation of wisdom from various books.

This book is a beacon for those yet to embark on a transformative spiritual journey that can reshape their life narratives. Arnell established the nonprofit "A Time To Change" to aid families impacted by addiction. Through family and teen groups, Codependency sessions, DWI/DUI counseling, and substance abuse support, she imparts her strength, wisdom, and hope to countless individuals nationwide.

Active within her church, Arnell has led Bible study classes for over 15 years, fostering spiritual growth. Her commitment extends to various programs such as Alcoholic Anonymous, Cocaine Anonymous, Debtors Anonymous, Al-Anon, and Overeater's Anonymous programs, guiding others toward freedom from addictions and compulsions. With 23 years of marriage, five children, and four grandchildren, she exemplifies strength, trust, and advocacy for inner-city families seeking recovery and health. Today, as a great-grandmother, Arnell continues to inspire transformation from within the community itself. Arnell can be reached at www.arnellevans.com.

Printed in the United States
by Baker & Taylor Publisher Services